D0454884

YEARLING BOOKS

Since 1966, Yearling has been the

leading name in classic and award-winning

literature for young readers.

With a wide variety of titles,

Yearling paperbacks entertain, inspire,

and encourage a love of reading.

VISIT

WWW.RANDOMHOUSE.COM/KIDS

**TO FIND THE PERFECT BOOK, PLAY GAMES,
AND MEET FAVORITE AUTHORS!**

OTHER YEARLING BOOKS YOU WILL ENJOY

BE FIRST IN THE UNIVERSE
Stephanie Spinner and Terry Bisson

I WAS A RAT!, *Philip Pullman*

THE PLAYMAKER, *J. B. Cheaney*

MIDWINTER NIGHTINGALE, *Joan Aiken*

KEY TO THE TREASURE, *Peggy Parish*

PIRATE ISLAND ADVENTURE, *Peggy Parish*

THE BOYS START THE WAR, *Phyllis Reynolds Naylor*

BAD GIRLS, *Jacqueline Wilson*

SAMMY KEYES AND THE HOLLYWOOD MUMMY
Wendelin Van Draanen

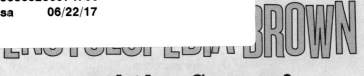

ENCYCLOPEDIA BROWN
and the Case of
Pablo's Nose

DONALD J. SOBOL

Illustrated by ERIC VELASQUEZ

A YEARLING BOOK

For my grandson,
Bryan Matthew Sobol

Published by Yearling, an imprint of Random House Children's Books
a division of Random House, Inc., New York

Visit us on the Web! www.randomhouse.com/kids

Educators and librarians, for a variety of teaching tools, visit us at
www.randomhouse.com/teachers

ISBN: 0-553-48513-X

Reprinted by arrangement with Delacorte Press

Printed in the United States of America

April 2003

20 19 18

Contents

The Case of the Sleeveless Lock

Idaville seemed no different from many other seaside towns.

It had lovely white beaches, a Little League, banks, churches, a synagogue, and two delicatessens.

Nevertheless, Idaville was different.

Very different. . . .

For more than a year no one, grown-up or child, had gotten away with breaking the law there.

How did Idaville do it? Police officers from coast to coast wondered. So did the CIA and the FBI. What was the secret? How did it happen?

Only three people knew, and they weren't telling.

All three lived in a redbrick house at 13 Rover Avenue— Mr. Brown, Mrs. Brown, and their only child, ten-year-old Encyclopedia, America's crime-buster in sneakers.

Mr. Brown was chief of police. He was honest, brave, and

smart. When he had a case that puzzled him, he always knew what to do.

He drove home.

Encyclopedia solved the case for him at the dinner table. Usually before dessert. Usually with one question.

Chief Brown wished he could tell the world about his son. But he knew it was useless. Who would believe him?

Who would believe that a fifth-grader was the mastermind behind Idaville's war on crime?

So Chief Brown didn't say a word. Neither did Mrs. Brown.

For his part, Encyclopedia never boasted about the help he gave his father. Boasting was for people who needed to feel important.

There was nothing, however, he could do about his nickname.

Only his parents and teachers called him by his real name, Leroy. Everyone else called him Encyclopedia.

An encyclopedia is a book or set of books filled with facts from A to Z. So was Encyclopedia's head. He had read more books than anybody, and he never forgot a word.

His pals said he was better than an encyclopedia. He was like a whole library that you could take along on a fishing trip.

Monday evening Chief Brown sat silently at the dinner table, staring at his cream of broccoli soup.

Mrs. Brown and Encyclopedia knew what was wrong. A case had him troubled.

"What sort of case is it, dear?" Mrs. Brown asked.

"One without a crime," Chief Brown answered. He stirred his soup for a moment.

Mrs. Brown and Encyclopedia waited patiently.

"John Long is getting married tomorrow," Chief Brown said. "He hoped to give his bride the wedding ring that his grandmother left him. He can't."

"He lost it?" asked Mrs. Brown.

"No," Chief Brown replied. "The ring is safe. In fact, it's altogether too safe."

He explained. The ring was kept in a safe in the home of John's uncle, Gordon Long, with whom John lived. The uncle was the only person who could open the safe.

"The uncle flew to Brazil shortly before John announced his wedding date," Chief Brown said. "He said he'd be back in a few days. He's already been gone two months. Brazil is a big country, and John doesn't know where to reach him."

"Why doesn't John postpone the wedding?" Mrs. Brown inquired. "Or use another ring?"

"John has had his heart set on using his grandmother's ring," Chief Brown said. "Besides, it's too late to postpone the wedding. Most of the out-of-town guests have already arrived in Idaville."

"The uncle must have hidden a spare key someplace," Mrs. Brown said.

"A spare key won't help," Chief Brown said. "The safe has a combination lock."

"This really isn't a police case," Mrs. Brown said. "How did you get into it?"

3

"I caught the thieves who robbed John's gas station last year," Chief Brown replied. "He asked me to help him again. I'm supposed to figure out how to open the safe. He said he didn't trust anyone else."

Encyclopedia had been sitting quietly, listening. He knew his father and mother were going over the case for his sake. They were trying to give him all the facts he needed to solve it.

Suddenly his mother straightened. "Isn't John's uncle that retired lawyer who is rather strange? He's always dashing around the world, photographing the longest of anything."

"That's right," Chief Brown said. "Already this year he has photographed the longest bathroom shelf and the longest cigar ash."

"I've heard," Mrs. Brown said, "that he has ten albums filled with photos of the longest of almost everything."

"I suppose everyone ought to have a hobby," Encyclopedia murmured.

"The uncle hoped to photograph the longest cockroach and the longest whatever else he can find in Brazil," Chief Brown said.

He put down his soup spoon before continuing.

"The safe with the ring in it is hidden behind a picture of the longest undershirt," he said. "On the safe itself, in the uncle's handwriting, is the word *sleeveless*."

"Why write *sleeveless*? It isn't the longest word," said Mrs. Brown, who had taught high-school English and other subjects. "The longest is a Greek word. In English, it has one hundred and eighty-two letters. The word is *lopadotemachisel* . . . oh, I can't remember the rest—"

She broke off. Encyclopedia had closed his eyes. He always closed his eyes when he did his hardest thinking.

When at last he opened his eyes, he asked his one question.

"Does the uncle have a poor memory?"

"Why, as a matter of fact, yes," Chief Brown said. "Not only can't he remember what he had for breakfast, he usually can't remember *where* he had it."

"I guess he got so busy in Brazil chasing down the longest things that he forgot the date of the wedding," Mrs. Brown said.

"But why did he write *sleeveless* on the safe?" Chief Brown said. "It's such a common, everyday word."

"Common, yet uncommon, Dad," Encyclopedia said.

Father and mother looked at their son questioningly.

Encyclopedia said, "The uncle wrote *sleeveless* on the safe because it's the longest example of a certain type of word. Every time he uses the safe, *sleeveless* reminds him of the combination."

Chief Brown knitted his brows thoughtfully. "Why didn't he simply write down the combination and keep it in his wallet or in a drawer?"

"Because it might fall out of his wallet," Encyclopedia said. "If he hid it somewhere, he might forget where."

"Leroy!" cried Mrs. Brown. "What is the combination to the safe?"

"Tell us," said Chief Brown, "before John gets married tomorrow! He wants to use his grandmother's ring so badly!"

Encyclopedia smiled.

Softly he said, "The combination to the safe is—"

What Is the Combination?

**(Turn to page 64 for the solution to
The Case of the Sleeveless Lock.)**

The Case of the Smoke Signals

Besides helping his father solve mysteries, Encyclopedia helped the children of the neighborhood.

When school let out for the summer, he opened his own detective agency in the garage. Every morning after breakfast he hung out his sign:

Brown Detective Agency
13 Rover Avenue
LEROY BROWN
President
No case too small
25¢ a day plus expenses

The first customer Tuesday was Muriel Rivers. Her hobby was Native American customs and crafts. Her favorite tribes were the Creek and the Susquehanna.

"I want to hire you," she said, and handed Encyclopedia twenty-five cents. "Bugs Meany cheated me."

Bugs Meany was the leader of a gang of tough older boys. They called themselves the Tigers. They should have called themselves the Pots and Pans. They were always cooking up trouble.

Encyclopedia stayed busy keeping Bugs from bullying the little kids of the neighborhood.

"How did Bugs cheat you?" Encyclopedia inquired.

"He took my totem pole," Muriel said.

She explained. About eight o'clock the night before, she had been returning home with a little totem pole she had bought at the Museum of Natural History gift shop. Bugs had stopped her. He said he'd trade her a how-to booklet on smoke signals for the totem pole.

"Like an airhead, I agreed," Muriel said. "Bugs took my totem pole and promised to leave the booklet at my door. What he left was a booklet on smoking a pipe."

"Did you try to get back the totem pole?" the detective asked.

"Sure, but Bugs did all the talking," Muriel replied. "He told me to read the booklet and buy a peace pipe. He said I had to start small. Then he told me to get lost."

"Let's go see Bugs," Encyclopedia said.

"Include me out," Muriel said. "Bugs said if I came around again he'd shove me into a mustard jar. I'll stay right here, even if I have to force myself."

"Don't be afraid," Encyclopedia said. "Bugs's belch is worse than his bite. Thinking gives him a headache."

Muriel shrugged. "Okay, I'll go along, but I wish I had a survival kit."

The Tigers' clubhouse was an empty toolshed behind Mr. Sweeney's auto body shop. Bugs was outside with Monk Walsh, one of his Tigers.

"Man oh man!" Bugs growled upon seeing Encyclopedia and Muriel. "Look what came out of the rain forest!"

Encyclopedia was used to Bugs's greetings. "You know Muriel Rivers, I believe," he said calmly.

"Yeah," Bugs answered. "Not a bad kid if looks and brains don't count."

"Did you promise to give her a booklet on smoke signals in return for her totem pole?" Encyclopedia asked.

Bugs raised his nose. "It's true that I'm a master at sending smoke signals. I say this humbly. But totem pole? Booklet? Why, the girl has drunk too many milk shakes."

"Is that so?" Muriel cried. "Where were you last night around eight?"

Bugs blinked. "Uh . . . me and Monk were in South Park making smoke signals."

Muriel snorted. "Liar!"

"We'll show you where we were," Monk shot back.

They all biked to the park's picnic grounds, a grassy area with tables, benches, and barbecue grills.

On the east side of the grounds was a lake. On the west side was a little forest of oak trees. On the other two sides were a parking area and a baseball field.

Bugs walked up to a grill. It had ashes in it.

"We used this very grill last night to practice sending smoke signals," he said. "Us Tigers respect the land. We don't build fires on the ground like lawbreakers."

Encyclopedia was thinking over what he knew about smoke signals. Native Americans had used them mostly as warnings. A sudden puff told of strangers on the plain below. Quick puffs meant the strangers were well armed. If smoke was allowed to rise steadily, it meant the tribe had to gather its warriors for battle.

Bugs said, "We came here last night because there was no wind and no one was around. We don't like to bother anyone or be bothered."

"No one was around," Encyclopedia said, "because the picnic area is closed on weekdays after sundown."

"We forgot it was Monday. Is that a crime?" Bugs said.

"How come you didn't get caught?" Muriel asked. "The police patrol to make sure no one is up to mischief. They use searchlights."

Bugs grinned. "We saw a searchlight. It scared us, I'll admit. We ran."

"The searchlights are on the police cars," Muriel said.

The news rocked Bugs back on his heels and made Monk's ears wiggle.

"Tell me you outran a police car!" Muriel challenged.

Bugs steadied himself. "The searchlight we saw turned out to be the full moon shining through the oak forest over there."

"There *was* a full moon last night," Muriel murmured to

Encyclopedia. "Bugs has all the answers, even though he's lying through his teeth. It's his word against mine."

"Not quite," Encyclopedia said.

What Was Bugs's Mistake?

(Turn to page 65 for the solution to The Case of the Smoke Signals.)

The Case of the Peace Offering

The mind of Bugs Meany burned with a mighty longing—to get even with Encyclopedia Brown.

Bugs hated being outsmarted all the time. He longed to leave the detective with plenty to give the tooth fairy.

But Bugs never used muscle. Whenever he felt like it, he remembered Sally Kimball. She was Encyclopedia's junior partner in the detective agency.

Sally was more than the prettiest girl in the fifth grade and the best athlete. She had done what no little kid had believed possible.

Flattened Bugs Meany.

Whenever they fought, Bugs hit the ground as if he were proving the law of gravity.

"Bugs won't rest till he gets back at us," Sally warned. "He's trouble."

Encyclopedia sighed. "Bugs is his own worst enemy."

"Not while I'm alive," Sally snapped.

The detectives were walking to Bugs's house. The Tigers' leader had invited them over that morning.

"Let's let bygones be bygones," he had purred. "I've got an electric drill for you. Call it a peace offering. Stop by my house at noon, okay? Meet me inside the garage."

The garage was open when the detectives reached it at noon. They went inside. Bugs wasn't there.

"I don't like this," Sally said. "Bugs is pulling one of his dirty tricks. Why would he want to give us an electric drill?"

"I don't know," Encyclopedia said. "But we agreed to see what he's up to. He may really want to be friends."

"Maybe you're right," Sally sighed. "There's the electric drill in the wheelbarrow."

She had just picked it up when Bugs charged through the door from the kitchen. He whistled between his fingers.

Mr. McCann, who lived next door, came into the garage on the run. He halted and stared at the electric drill in Sally's hands. "So *you're* the ones," he gasped in disbelief.

"Caught red-handed!" roared Bugs. "Detectives, my foot! All that goody-good act is nothing but a cover for a life of crime!"

"What's going on?" Sally demanded.

"A lot of tools have been stolen from garages in the neighborhood lately," Mr. McCann replied.

"The robbers always choose a house where the garage door has been left open," Bugs said.

"Bugs told me that two hours ago he had a power failure and couldn't close the electric garage door," Mr. McCann said. "His folks are away, and so he asked me come over if he whistled for help."

16

"Look at them! Caught like rats in a trap!" Bugs sang, dancing with glee. "This is the happiest day of my life—except the day I was born."

"I'm going to call your parents," Mr. McCann told the detectives, and returned to his house.

Encyclopedia walked to a metal box on the wall. Inside were the circuit breakers that turned on or off the flow of electricity throughout the house.

"Number six is off," he said. "What rooms does it control?"

"The garage and the kitchen," Bugs said. "If there's a problem in any line, the proper switch turns it off."

"Or you can turn it off yourself," Encyclopedia added.

He pushed the number six switch on.

"Funny you didn't close the garage door by hand," he said. "All you have to do is jerk the unlocking chain up there to break the connection."

Bugs smiled slyly. "I never got the hang of circuit breakers or electric garage doors."

"Mind if I check the kitchen?" Encyclopedia asked.

Bugs sneered. "Be my guest."

In the kitchen the detective flipped a wall switch. The light above the breakfast table went on.

On the table stood a can of soda. Beside it on a paper plate was the thickest sandwich Encyclopedia had ever seen. Between two pieces of white toast were layers of ham, salami, liverwurst, cheese, lettuce, and tomato.

"I'd just finished making my lunch," Bugs said, "when I heard you in the garage."

"You *framed* us," Sally accused him. "Tell Mr. McCann the truth or you'll be sorry."

"Ask a Tiger to tell a lie? I ought to give you this," Bugs said, raising a fist.

"What's in it?" Sally asked.

Bugs came to a fast boil. "I've always gone easy on you, you smart skirt. Now it's fight time for real!"

"So fight," Sally said, and stuck out her chin.

Bugs flew into a rage. He forgot whom he was up against and lunged wildly, trying to get in the first punch.

Sally ducked. "Sock-a-doodle-do," she cooed, and fired a one-two to the chops.

Suddenly Bugs was not feeling like himself. He walked around like a dumb squirrel trying to remember where he'd hidden the acorns.

Sally fed him a stiff left.

Bugs landed on his back. After a few gurgles and twitches, he lifted his head and looked around goofy-eyed.

"Whose buffalo was that?" he moaned.

Sally rubbed her knuckles. "Encyclopedia, we still have to *prove* that Bugs tried to frame us."

"No we don't," Encyclopedia said. "Bugs proved it for us."

What Was the Proof?

**(Turn to page 66 for the solution to
The Case of the Peace Offering.)**

The Case of the Masked Man

Sunday morning the detectives heard strange noises as they walked past Professor Irvin's house.

Sally stopped. "Someone is in trouble."

"Maybe it's just a pooch beating its tail on the floor," Encyclopedia offered hopefully.

"That's thumping," Sally said. "This is stamping. We'd better check it out."

Encyclopedia wished Sally were a little less fond of checking things out. Professor Irvin, who taught American history at State University, was a smart man. He could take care of himself.

Sally walked to the front door. It was unlocked.

She poked her head in. "Is anyone home?"

The stamping grew faster and louder.

The detectives stepped inside.

"Professor Irvin?" Sally called. "Are you all right?"

The stamping grew even faster and louder.

Sally pointed to a closed door. "It's coming from in there."

She pushed the door open a crack, and then all the way.

Encyclopedia looked into a room walled with bookshelves. A woman sat in a chair in front of a desk. She was bound and gagged.

The detectives quickly freed her.

"Call the police!" she wailed. "Professor Irvin has been kidnapped!"

Encyclopedia sped to the telephone on the desk and made the call.

"The police will be here in a few minutes," he reported.

The woman had risen to her feet. She stretched her limbs and rubbed the soreness from her wrists.

"Every time I heard someone passing the house, I stamped on the floor," she said. "Thank heaven you children caught on. My legs were about to give out."

"Who are you, ma'am?" Encyclopedia asked politely.

"Mrs. Witten. I'm Professor Irvin's secretary." She pulled out a small handkerchief, wiped her eyes, blew her nose, and told them what had happened.

Half an hour ago she'd been making coffee in the kitchen when a masked gunman entered through the back door. He marched her to the den. Professor Irvin was at his desk.

"As the masked man was tying me up," she said, "he noticed Professor Irvin writing on a sheet of paper. The professor explained that he was only making notes for a speech."

"What then?" Sally asked.

"The masked man grabbed the sheet of paper," Mrs. Wit-

22

ten said. "He read it, threw it into the wastebasket, and tied the professor's hands behind his back."

She paused to blow her nose again.

"The horrible creature," she continued, "told me that the ransom for Professor Irvin would be half a million dollars. The money must be ready by tomorrow, when he'll phone with instructions. He took the professor away at gunpoint!"

"Half a million dollars!" Sally gasped. "Who can raise that much so quickly?"

"Professor Irvin's family," Mrs. Witten said. "They have a lot of money."

Encyclopedia went to the wastebasket and removed its contents—a shoe ad and a sheet of paper.

On the sheet was written a list of names: Washington, Jefferson, Lincoln, Jackson, and Grant.

"Did you notice anything special about the kidnapper?" Encyclopedia inquired.

"His voice," Mrs. Witten replied. "I've heard it before, but I can't remember where."

Encyclopedia passed the sheet to Sally.

"The names of five Presidents," she murmured. "How could the professor do it? Mrs. Witten was being tied to a chair right in front of him, and he calmly made notes for a speech!"

"I don't believe the names are notes for a speech," Encyclopedia said. "I think they are a code that tells who the kidnapper is. The professor must have recognized him despite the mask."

Sally stared at the list. "All these Presidents held office during a war, or fought in one, didn't they?"

"All except Jefferson," Encyclopedia corrected.

To Mrs. Witten he said, "Would you know the kidnapper if you had a name to go with his voice?"

"I'm sure I would," she answered.

"Is it Jefferson?" Sally suggested eagerly.

"I'm sorry," Mrs. Witten said. "I'm afraid not."

Sally wrinkled her nose. "The names must be notes for a speech after all."

"No," Encyclopedia declared. "Professor Irvin wouldn't dare write down the kidnapper's name for him to see. My guess is that the professor invented a code on the spot."

Encyclopedia closed his eyes. He was thinking his hardest.

After a while he opened his eyes. "Got it!" he exclaimed. "The code should have *six* names! The kidnapper must have grabbed the sheet before Professor Irvin had time to write the sixth name."

"What is the sixth name, young man?" Mrs. Witten said.

"Franklin."

"Encyclopedia!" cried Sally. "Is Franklin the kidnapper's name? Is it?"

"No," said Encyclopedia. "The kidnapper's name is the name that Professor Irvin had time to write down, but purposely didn't."

What Was the Kidnapper's Name?

(Turn to page 67 for the solution to The Case of the Masked Man.)

The Case of the Organ-Grinder

Encyclopedia and Sally nearly tripped over Tony Gerosa in the Sunland Shopping Center.

Tony was on his hands and knees. He was staring into a tin cup held by a toy monkey dressed in a cute suit. The monkey stood atop a hand organ.

"What's wrong, Tony?" Sally asked.

Tony made a noise like a stepped-on chicken. Then he stammered, "K-Kome sid stole my coins."

"How's that?" Encyclopedia said.

"Some kid, I mean," Tony said, and tried again. "Some kid stole my coins."

He explained. The hand organ belonged to his grandfather, a retired organ-grinder. Tony had borrowed it to raise money for his club's flag football team.

"We need flags and a football," he said.

"What are you doing on the floor?" asked Encyclopedia.

Tony tapped the water fountain by his shoulder.

"A minute ago I went for a drink," he said. "I can't bend over with the organ on my stomach. So I set it on the floor. A boy ran off with all the money in the cup—nearly five dollars!"

"Gosh, business was good," Sally said.

"I get a lot of coins from people who pay me to stop playing," Tony admitted.

"What did the thief look like?" Encyclopedia asked.

Tony became excited all over again. "He wore a tight wee-shirt. I mean, a white T-shirt."

He couldn't get the next words out.

"Take your time," Sally said.

She leaned forward and put her ear close to his lips.

Tony whispered with difficulty.

"The thief might still be nearby," Encyclopedia said hopefully.

"If I were he, I'd get as far away as I could," Sally declared. "He probably headed straight home."

"Uh-uh," Encyclopedia disagreed. "He has Tony's money. He'll want to spend it."

"I'll hire you to find him, but I can't go with you," Tony said. "I've got money to raise."

He strapped on the hand organ and turned the crank. Out spilled "Pop Goes the Weasel."

"Nowadays a lot of hand organs use tape-recorded music, but not Grandpa's," Tony said proudly. "It can play six tunes."

A woman dropped a coin into the cup. Tony pressed a button on the organ. The toy monkey tipped its hat.

"Grandpa worked with a real monkey till people complained it was cruel," Tony said.

He stopped cranking for a moment.

"I wish I could be more help," he apologized. "But that boy was into my cup and gone so fast!"

"We'll find him," Encyclopedia promised.

"The T-shirt is a really good clue," Sally said.

As they moved off, Encyclopedia asked Sally, "What was on the T-shirt?"

"Tony said the words POLAR BEARS were written across the chest," Sally answered.

The detectives began searching the shopping center for a boy who wore a white T-shirt with the words POLAR BEARS.

Suddenly Sally squeezed Encyclopedia's arm.

"Over there," she murmured.

A boy in a white T-shirt stood in front of a toy store. He turned around, and Sally groaned with disappointment.

Written on his T-shirt was BE DIFFERENT—ACT NORMAL.

White T-shirts were everywhere, but not always with a boy inside and never with POLAR BEARS outside.

In a sporting goods store the detectives came up behind a boy in a white T-shirt carrying a small brown paper bag.

"There could be five dollars' worth of something in the bag," Sally said.

They cut in front of the boy, only to be disappointed again. On his T-shirt were the words KING PIN BOWLER.

"Have you noticed something?" Sally said. "There are so many people wearing T-shirts with words like BOWLING or BOWLER written on them."

"The state bowling tournament begins at the Ocean Lanes tomorrow," Encyclopedia said. "Idaville is full of bowlers."

"Even little kids?" Sally said. She pointed to a girl with WEST SIDE BOWLING PAIRS on her T-shirt.

"The tournament has age groups," Encyclopedia said. "The younger kids bowl in teams of two, or pairs."

In a hat shop they saw a boy with GUTTER BALL on his T-shirt. At a candy counter were three boys with ROOM TO SPARE, BOWLER PAIRS, and TIME TO SPLIT on their white T-shirts.

The detectives continued searching.

They saw short boys and tall boys, skinny boys and fat boys. None had POLAR BEARS on his T-shirt.

"If only Tony had gotten a good look at the thief's face," Sally grumbled.

They reached the end of the shopping center.

"Let's give it up," Sally said. "It's hopeless."

"We took the case, and we'll finish it," Encyclopedia insisted. "We're not quitting."

Sally flinched. "As Tony would say, I'll soon have fired teet."

Encyclopedia stopped in his tracks.

"Sally, that's it!" he exclaimed. "The thief is—"

Who Was the Thief?

(Turn to page 68 for the solution to The Case of the Organ-Grinder.)

31

The Case of Pablo's Nose

Pablo Pizzaro, Idaville's greatest boy artist, burst into the Brown Detective Agency.

"My nose," he wailed. "It's been stolen!"

"Whoever stole it returned it in very good shape," Sally observed.

"I don't mean *my* nose," Pablo said. "I mean Abraham Lincoln's."

He explained. Last month the nose on the statue of Abraham Lincoln in South Park had been smashed to pieces by a baseball. So the mayor had announced a New Nose Now contest. The winning nose would be put on the statue. The winning sculptor would get a cash prize.

"I thought I had a good chance of nosing out everyone else," Pablo said proudly, and told why.

First he had made a mold of the statue's face. Then, using

33

photographs of Abraham Lincoln, he had built a nose in soft wax. Next he had ground down a piece of the same stone from which the statue had been carved to make sure he had the right texture and color. Then he had mixed that with his special glue. Finally he had shaped the mixture into a copy of the wax model.

"Golly, Pablo!" Sally exclaimed. "You're a regular plastic surgeon!"

Pablo smiled a weak smile. "The nose was my masterpiece," he said. "There isn't time to make another. The contest ends Thursday."

"Are you sure it was stolen?" Encyclopedia asked.

"Sure I'm sure," Pablo said. "I've been leaving the nose on the front lawn to weather so it would make an even better match with Lincoln's face."

Half an hour ago, he went on, he had discovered that the nose was gone. At the same time he'd noticed a girl biking away from his house like mad. She'd been holding something the size of the nose in her right hand.

"Did you see who she was?" Sally asked.

"I only saw her back," Pablo said sadly. "She wore a blue shirt and rode a purple bicycle."

He paused for a strengthening breath of air.

"I should have kept my nose a secret," he muttered. "Like a blockhead, I bragged all over the neighborhood."

He laid a quarter on the gas can beside Encyclopedia.

"Find my nose!" he pleaded.

"There are three purple bicycles in the neighborhood,"

Sally said. "Desmoana Lowry has one. So do Martha Katz and Joan Brand."

The detectives and Pablo started at Martha Katz's house. From Mrs. Katz they learned that Martha was spending the summer with her grandparents in Maine.

The news was no better at Joan Brand's house. Joan had gone off to Camp Winiwantoc in North Carolina a week ago.

"That leaves Desmoana Lowry," Sally said.

"She has to be the thief," Pablo said. "She's been jealous of me since I beat her in the tulip drawing contest last year."

"Being jealous isn't being a thief," Encyclopedia said quietly. "Let's pay her a visit."

Desmoana came to the front door herself. "What do you want?" she demanded, giving Pablo an unfriendly look.

Pablo accused her straightaway. "About an hour ago, you stole my nose, didn't you?"

"No, but I should have," Desmoana retorted. "I'd have improved your looks."

"He means Abraham Lincoln's nose," Sally said. "The thief wore a blue shirt and rode a purple bicycle."

"Does this look like a blue shirt?" Desmoana asked.

The shirt she had on looked very red to Encyclopedia.

"You could have changed your shirt," Sally said. "But you can't have repainted your purple bicycle in an hour."

"I didn't need to," Desmoana retorted. "I didn't steal anything."

She led the detectives and Pablo to the garage. A purple bicycle stood half hidden behind the water heater.

"When was the last time anyone saw me ride my bike?" she said. "Not for a long time, right? Fact is, it hasn't been ridden for nearly a year."

"That's the most unheard-of thing I ever heard of!" Pablo yelped.

Sally seemed uncertain. She glanced nervously at Encyclopedia.

Encyclopedia was uncertain, too. He tried to recall when he'd seen Desmoana on her bike last.

It was a bad moment.

Then a happy thought struck him.

"Why did you try to hide your bicycle?" he asked.

"I wasn't hiding it," Desmoana replied. "I put it out of the way. I'm into roller skating now. It's more fun."

"That's not the reason," Encyclopedia said. "Come on, tell the truth. You were never much good at riding a two-wheeler."

"Who says?" Desmoana snapped.

She rolled the purple bicycle out to the street.

"Slam your eyes on this," she invited, and forthwith did some trick riding.

She rode in a circle no-handed.

She sat on the handlebars and pedaled backward.

She lifted the front wheel off the ground and whipped through a figure eight.

"There!" she sneered. "I showed you how I can ride a two-wheeler."

"You showed me, all right," Encyclopedia agreed. "You showed me you're guilty!"

How Did Encyclopedia Know?

**(Turn to page 69 for the solution to
The Case of Pablo's Nose.)**

The Case of the Carousel Horse

The morning after Pablo Pizzaro won the New Nose Now contest, he came bouncing into the Brown Detective Agency.

"I'm headed for the big time," he announced. "Caldwell Jones asked me to be his helper this summer!"

Caldwell Jones was a sculptor. He had come from England last year and settled in Idaville.

"Wow! What a great summer job," Encyclopedia said.

"You'll earn while you learn," added Sally. "I hope."

Pablo frowned. "I forgot to ask about my pay."

"You'd better ask," Sally said firmly.

Pablo put twenty-five cents on the gas can by Encyclopedia. "I'm due at Mr. Jones's place in half an hour. Come with me. I might need someone with a good business head."

"We'll help you anyway we can," Encyclopedia promised.

"I've never seen a real artist's studio," Sally said in a dreamy voice.

Mr. Jones lived in the old part of Idaville. The children found him sitting on his porch.

"I brought my friends along," Pablo said, introducing the detectives. "Could they see your studio?"

"Of course," Mr. Jones boomed from somewhere within his thick red beard. "Come inside."

The studio was a large room filled with wood carvings, tools, stools, and tables. It smelled like a cigar box. Wood chips and slops of paint and varnish covered the floor.

"The place needs a good cleaning," Mr. Jones said, looking at Pablo.

"Leave it to me," Pablo replied, though rather feebly.

"I say, you'll do dashing well," Mr. Jones said approvingly. "Now let me show you something rare and beautiful."

He walked to an object as big as a piece of furniture, hidden under a bedsheet.

"Behold!" Mr. Jones said, pulling off the sheet.

Encyclopedia beheld a white wooden horse. Its saddle and blanket were painted in bright colors. Red roses bloomed in its golden mane.

"I call him Emperor," Mr. Jones said. "The hole behind the neck is for the pole. Emperor was made for a carousel. How I wish I'd carved him! Can you guess who did?"

Sally and Pablo shook their heads. Encyclopedia searched his memory.

"I'll give you a clue," Mr. Jones said.

He ran a finger alongside a small painting just above the raised left front leg. "President Teddy Roosevelt."

"There was a carver who always painted President Roosevelt's face on his horses," Encyclopedia said thoughtfully.

Mr. Jones's eyebrows shot up in surprise. "Very good, young man," he said. "Now look there."

He pointed to a name carved just below the picture of President Roosevelt: R. A. Bently.

"Bently was the leading carousel carver in America," Mr. Jones said. "His horses were so lifelike they almost seemed able to gallop off the carousel platform."

"Why did he always put a picture of President Roosevelt on his horses?" Sally inquired.

"Pictures and other decorations often appeared on the finer horses," Mr. Jones replied. "Bently probably liked President Roosevelt because they were born on the same day, October twenty-seventh, 1858."

Pablo had walked to the far side of the horse.

"This side doesn't have a picture, or writing, or nearly as much carving," he said, puzzled. "How come?"

"The inner side of wood carousel figures were always plain," Mr. Jones explained. "The side facing the onlookers had the pictures and fancy carvings."

"I seem to remember that Bently made very few horses," Encyclopedia remarked.

"Right again," Mr. Jones said. "Bently carved only six horses, all different. We know nothing more about him than that he worked for the William Mangels Company. Not one photograph of his horses exists."

He gazed at Emperor for a moment.

"The age of the wooden horse is past," he said sadly. "There will be no more masterpieces like Emperor. Today carousel animals are cast in fiberglass, any number of them alike. Saves money."

"What happened to Bently's other horses?" Pablo asked.

"They were smashed when a hurricane hit Florida," Mr. Jones said. "Only Emperor survived."

He paused to stroke Emperor's back.

"I was walking in Miami last November," he went on, "when I spotted a wooden horse on a front porch. He was pretty beat up. Yet something about his lines made me stop and take a closer look. Roosevelt's picture and Bently's name were faded but there!"

"How exciting!" Sally exclaimed.

"I couldn't believe my good luck," Mr. Jones said. "The owner had no use for the old horse anymore. Her children had played on him, but they were all grown up. She was glad to sell him to me."

"How long did it take you to make him look like new?" Pablo asked.

"Months," Mr. Jones said. "It was a labor of love."

"Emperor must be worth a lot of money now," Sally said.

Mr. Jones whistled through his red beard. "The one remaining Bently horse? He's worth his weight in diamonds."

"Mr. Jones knows so much," Sally whispered. "Pablo is lucky to land a job with him."

"Not if honesty is important," Encyclopedia whispered back.

What Did Encyclopedia Mean?

(Turn to page 70 for the solution to The Case of the Carousel Horse.)

The Case of the Wilford Whammy

Fifi O'Brien burst into the Brown Detective Agency.

"I'm going to be so rich I'll be able to live beyond my wildest dreams!" she exclaimed.

"Who said so?" asked Sally.

"Wilford Wiggins."

Encyclopedia sighed heavily. "Wilford never gives up."

Wilford Wiggins was a high-school dropout and as lazy as a bedpost. He spent his days dreaming up ways to part little kids from their savings.

He never got a nickel, however. Encyclopedia always stopped his phony deals in time.

Only last week Wilford had tried to peddle chicken feed made from ground-up electric mixers. After eating just half a pound of feed, he said, a hen would lay scrambled eggs.

"Wilford has called a secret meeting at the city dump for five o'clock today," Fifi said.

"What's he selling now?" Sally inquired. "A sauce that makes space suits taste like pot roast?"

"Wilford didn't say," Fifi replied. "But he promised to make us little kids so rich our banks will beg for mercy."

"Wilford is long on promises but so short on memory he thinks he's honest," Encyclopedia said.

"This time is different," Fifi insisted. "Wilford told me he isn't lying anymore. I believe him. He hates liars."

"Is that why he goes around swearing at himself?" Sally snapped.

Fifi suddenly looked troubled.

"I'd better hire you," she said, handing Encyclopedia a quarter. "I want you to make sure whatever Wilford is selling today is more than fast talk."

"If we're going to help, we better hurry," Sally said. "It's nearly five o'clock."

Wilford was standing beside a beat-up kitchen chair when the detectives and Fifi arrived at the city dump.

"Gather round," he called to the crowd of small children, "and bring your ears. I don't want any of my young friends to miss this chance of a lifetime!"

The children moved closer. They were eager to hear his newest shortcut to Easy Street.

Wilford threw up his hands. "Crime is rising every day. If it keeps going up, we'll all be criminals."

"Aw, lay off the laughs!" a boy hollered. "Show us your moneymaker."

"Right here, friend, right here," Wilford said.

From under his shirt he pulled a black tube.

His voice rose with excitement. "You're thinking this is just a flashlight. No way! It only looks like a flashlight. That is the beauty of it. A mugger won't suspect a thing until it's too late."

He peered at the ring of children.

"What is it, you ask? It's the Wilford Whammy! To show you its amazing power, I need a volunteer."

No one raised a hand.

"I won't hurt you," Wilford called. "Trust me."

A blond boy whom Encyclopedia had never seen before pushed forward. "How about me, motormouth?"

"You'll do," Wilford answered coolly. "Make believe you have a knife. Demand all my cash."

"Gimme your wallet," the boy said, speaking as if he meant it.

Wilford whipped the Wilford Whammy against the boy's forehead.

"I can't move," the boy croaked.

Wilford quickly withdrew the Wilford Whammy. The boy shook his head and slunk away, meek as an off-duty cow.

"You saw for yourself," Wilford sang. "The Wilford Whammy zapped him silly faster than you can hiccup!"

"Baloney!" shouted Fifi. "Try it on someone we know. Try it on me."

Her challenge appeared to startle Wilford, but he gathered himself quickly. "I don't use it on girls," he said.

The other children jeered. They also hissed, hooted, and howled until Wilford gave in.

"Okay, okay," he said. "Better sit on this chair, little girl. I don't want you falling off your feet and cracking your pretty skull."

Fifi sat down.

"Chin up, head back, that's it," Wilford said as he pressed the Wilford Whammy to her forehead. "I'll only use half power. Go on, stand up."

Fifi could not stand up.

"Oh, you better mousetrap, move over!" Wilford roared in triumph.

The crowd of children stared wide-eyed as he removed the Wilford Whammy.

"I'll be honest with you," Wilford confessed. "I need money to build a factory. So I'm going to let my little pals buy shares in the Wilford Whammy for five dollars a share. The more shares you buy, the more money you'll make!"

"It really works," Fifi muttered as she came back to the detectives. "I couldn't get up."

"Think of it!" Wilford crowed. "You can own a part of the Wilford Whammy company! While my little beauty is fighting crime and protecting your loved ones, it will be making you millions!"

The children looked at one another. Did Wilford say *millions*?

Greed overcame doubt. They lined up to buy shares.

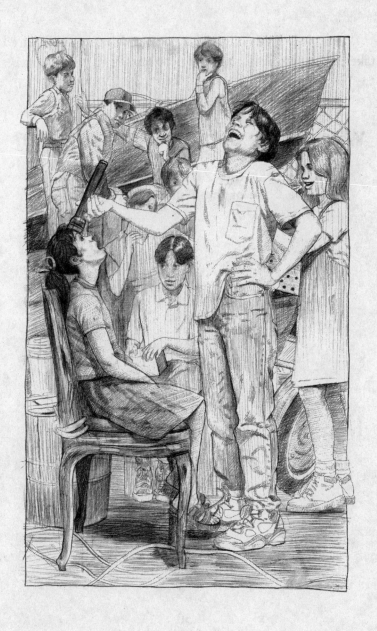

"Encyclopedia," Sally said, "do something before Wilford takes all their savings. You can, can't you?"

"Of course," said Encyclopedia.

What Made Encyclopedia So Sure?

(Turn to page 71 for the solution to The Case of the Wilford Whammy.)

The Case of the Racing Reptiles

Wednesday morning Encyclopedia and Sally went over to Barry Duncan's house. They wanted to see his two racing lizards, Erasmus and Erastus.

Barry had been telling everyone what fast steppers Erasmus and Erastus were. He was training them for Idaville's Great Snake, Turtle, and Lizard Races on Saturday.

When the detectives arrived, Barry was standing in his driveway with Spike Larson, one of Bugs Meany's Tigers. The two boys were jawing at each other, nose to nose and toe to toe.

Encyclopedia couldn't hear what was being said. But it was a cinch they weren't asking each other over for tea.

"Uh-oh, I better break this up before Barry gets hurt," Sally said.

She hurried across the street. Encyclopedia followed uneasily.

Spike saw them approaching.

"Stay out of this, you gumballs," he warned. "Go somewhere and adopt a pig."

Sally didn't scare. "What's going on?" she demanded.

"Spike let Kid Tiger, his snake, slip into the cage with Erasmus and Erastus," Barry said. "That snake ate them for breakfast!"

"Liar!" Spike roared. "Remember what your face looks like because I'm going to change it."

"Ease off, Spike," Encyclopedia ordered, and edged closer to Sally. Spike had learned the hard way what she could do to a Tiger.

"Suppose you tell us exactly what happened," Sally suggested. "You first, Barry."

"Lizards are cold-blooded," Barry began. "In the morning I take Erasmus and Erastus outside and leave them in the cage. I let the sun warm them up to get them moving."

In the driveway was an empty cage. Its bars shone in the sunlight. From the small door on the side hung a closed lock.

Barry said, "After some time in the sun, Erasmus and Erastus are ready for their workout."

"Wherever do you get racing lizards?" Sally inquired.

"I found them near Mill Pond two weeks ago," Barry answered. "There are plenty of big lizards there. Erasmus and Erastus were the hardest to catch. So I knew they were faster than the average lizard.

"The races on Saturday," he went on, "will be held on a sixteen-foot ramp with a six-inch wall on both sides. My dad built a training ramp like it in the backyard. I get Erasmus and Erastus started by yelling and blowing on them."

"Which one is faster?" Sally asked.

"Erasmus wins if he rolls," Barry said. "Erastus is faster

afoot, but I can't count on him. Sometimes he jumps the wall for a side trip in the grass."

"Did you actually see Kid Tiger in the cage?" Encyclopedia inquired.

"You know it," Barry declared. "Half an hour ago I came out of the house. Kid Tiger had eaten Erasmus and was finishing off Erastus. He got away before I could catch him."

Sally said, "The lizards might have escaped through the door of the cage and still be alive. Another snake might have wandered in when the cage was empty."

"I know Kid Tiger when I see him," Barry said. "Besides, the door is always locked. I have the only key."

"Go on," Spike jeered. "Your story is gripping me."

"If you had fed that dumb snake, he wouldn't have been hungry!" Barry shot back.

"Oh, yeah?" Spike snarled. "If you bit your lip you'd die of food poisoning."

"Where is your snake now, Spike?" Sally put in quickly.

Spike pointed with his thumb over his shoulder. "At home."

He led them down the block to his house. In a small, open shed in the backyard there was a large glass tank.

Encyclopedia saw a boa constrictor, a Burmese python, and a family of harmless grass snakes.

He did not see Spike's black-and-yellow snake.

"My folks love all sorts of reptiles," Spike said. "They gave me Kid Tiger for a pet."

Suddenly he gasped. "Kid Tiger! He's gone!"

"You said a mouthful," Barry declared. "That snake is in the grass somewhere. He's sleeping off his big meal."

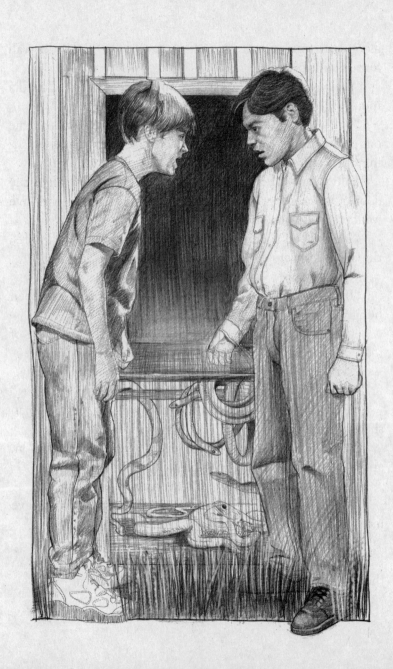

"You stole Kid Tiger so he couldn't beat your two Jurassic junk heaps tomorrow," Spike growled.

"Snakes don't race against lizards," Sally pointed out.

"Right," Barry said. "There are prizes for the winning snake, lizard, and turtle. But a grand prize goes to the kid whose racer is judged the best overall. Spike couldn't stand the idea of Erasmus or Erastus being the big winner."

"I'm giving you fair warning," Spike said. "Return Kid Tiger, or you better be a fast healer."

The two boys fell to jawing again. Sally pulled Encyclopedia aside.

"Either one could be trying to keep the other from winning best overall," she said. "Barry could have hidden Kid Tiger and Erasmus and Erastus, with the idea of 'finding' the lizards just before the races and the snake just afterward. Spike could have hidden Kid Tiger after slipping him into the cage to eat Erasmus and Erastus."

Encyclopedia stared silently at the empty cage.

"Good grief, say something!" Sally exclaimed. "Who is lying? You know, don't you?"

"Yes, and I'm sorry to have taken so long with it," Encyclopedia apologized. "The liar is—"

Who Lied?

(Turn to page 72 for the solution to The Case of the Racing Reptiles.)

55

The Case of the Unknown Thief

Storm clouds hung in the night sky as Encyclopedia and Sally left the movie theater.

"We have plenty of time to catch the number six bus home," Sally said.

The detectives headed toward the bus stop on Main Street. They had walked half a block when the storm broke.

"Rubin's Fine Jewelers will still be open," Encyclopedia shouted. "We can duck in there and take a later bus. Mr. Rubin is a friend of Dad's."

The detectives ran through the rain. They were soaked when they reached the jewelry store.

Six customers were inside. Mr. Rubin was at the cash register in the rear. Two men, their backs to the detectives, stood at the counter in front of him.

One of the men wore a gray suit and carried a wooden

cane with an ivory handle. The other wore a brown suit and had an umbrella.

Outside, the storm grew worse. Suddenly the lights dimmed.

"Oh, no, the power is going!" a woman gasped.

A moment later the lights in the store and on the street went out.

Everyone talked at once.

"I can't see a thing."

"Sarah, where are you?"

"Over here. Where are you?"

"It's like a bats' cave in here."

"No, like the Tunnel of Love."

Laughter.

Someone bumped Encyclopedia. He heard the door open and close. He could not see who left.

Presently the rain let up. The power, however, remained out. Encyclopedia heard the shop door opening and closing as customers left in the darkness.

After a few minutes more the lights came back on. The store was empty except for the detectives, Mr. Rubin, and the customer in the brown suit.

On the counter near the two men lay a wallet.

"Yours, Mr. Bower?" Mr. Rubin asked the man in the brown suit.

"No," Mr. Bower replied. "There was a man in a gray suit standing beside me before the blackout. It's probably his."

"I remember him," Mr. Rubin said. "He wanted to know if I could fix a watch while he waited. He put a watch on the

counter and took out his wallet. I was busy with you, and I didn't really look at him."

"Neither did I," said Mr. Bower.

Encyclopedia and Sally moved nearer. Mr. Rubin greeted them and picked up the wallet.

"No pictures, no driver's license, no credit cards," he muttered.

"What about money?" Mr. Bower said. "You better count it while I'm here. The owner might say he had more money in his wallet than there is."

Mr. Rubin nodded. He removed the bills one by one.

First he took out three one-dollar bills kept flat in the wallet. Next he took out two five-dollar bills. They were folded in half crosswise so that they were about three inches long. A ten-dollar bill was folded in thirds crosswise, making it about two inches long.

At the bottom of the wallet was a twenty-dollar bill. It was folded in half lengthwise.

"Forty-three dollars," Mr. Rubin said. "Wait . . . there is something else."

He dug out a small white strip of paper and studied it. Then he laid it on the counter for Mr. Bower and the detectives to read.

The slip was a cash register receipt dated a week ago. It was for $12.80 from Top Hardware Store down the street.

All at once Mr. Bower gasped. "Where is my watch?"

"Right here," Mr. Rubin said. "I hid it shortly after the lights went out."

He reached under the counter. "Good heavens!"

"What's the matter?" Mr. Bower asked.

Mr. Rubin had turned pale. "This is a woman's watch!"

Mr. Bower grabbed the watch. "That crook! He swapped watches when the lights went out. You can buy a better watch than this one at a drugstore."

Encyclopedia spoke quietly. "May I ask one question, Mr. Rubin?"

"Why . . . of course. Go ahead."

"While the man in the gray suit stood at the counter, did you mention how much Mr. Bower's watch was worth?"

"I may have," Mr. Rubin answered uncertainly. "It's such a fine, beautiful watch. Anyone can see that."

Mr. Bower picked up the receipt. "I'm going to take this to Top Hardware. Somebody may remember the sale."

"The sale was made last week," Sally said. "Who will remember a person who bought anything that long ago?"

"If I'd only taken the time to look at him," Mr. Rubin muttered.

"Don't worry," Encyclopedia said. "The thief probably lives close by, and he must do most of his shopping around here. So he isn't a stranger to the storekeepers. He won't be hard to find."

Mr. Rubin and Mr. Bower looked at the detective in amazement.

"How do you know so much about him?" Mr. Rubin demanded.

"Did you see who he was before the lights went out?" Mr. Bower asked.

"No," Encyclopedia answered, "but after the lights came back on, I saw the clue."

What Was the Clue?

(Turn to page 73 for the solution to
The Case of the Unknown Thief.)

Solutions

The Case of the Sleeveless Lock

The uncle had written *sleeveless* on his safe to help his poor memory.

Sleeveless was what he was always seeking: the longest example of something.

Sleeveless is the longest example of a pyramid word. A pyramid word has letters in rising order.

Sleeveless has one *v*, two *l*'s, three *s*'s, and four *e*'s.

Taking the number of times each letter appears in *sleeveless* and keeping them in the same order, *s-l-e-v*, allowed the uncle—and Encyclopedia—to come up with the combination: 3, 2, 4, 1.

The Case of the Smoke Signals

Muriel gave Bugs a problem. She asked how he had outrun a searchlight mounted on a police car.

Bugs had to come up with a fast answer. So he said he'd been mistaken. The searchlight he'd seen turned out to be the full moon shining behind the oak trees.

Impossible!

It was early in the evening, eight o'clock. So the moon would be rising. But the moon, like the sun and stars, rises in the *east* and sets in the west.

The oaks grew on the *west* side of the picnic grounds.

Bugs wasn't in the park at all that night.

Caught in his own mouthtrap, Bugs returned Muriel's totem pole. She gave back his pipe booklet.

The Case of the Peace Offering

Bugs used the thefts in garages around the neighborhood to frame Encyclopedia and Sally.

He opened his garage door. Then he got Mr. McCann to act as a witness by asking him to watch for thieves.

Bugs told Mr. McCann that the power had failed two hours ago, so the electric garage door could not be closed.

Bugs, of course, turned off the electricity himself. Encyclopedia spotted the proof in Bugs's lunch. The sandwich was made with white *toast*.

Bugs could not have used the toaster if the electricity had failed.

SOLUTION TO
The Case of the Masked Man

The quick-thinking Professor Irvin wrote down the names of men whose pictures appear on United States paper money in order of value.

That is: *Washington* ($1), *Jefferson* ($2), *Lincoln* ($5), *Jackson* ($20), and *Grant* ($50).

The kidnapper grabbed the list before the professor had time to complete it by writing *Franklin*. Benjamin Franklin's picture is on the $100 bill.

Nonetheless, the professor named his kidnapper—Hamilton—by leaving him off the list. Hamilton is on the $10 bill.

Police found Professor Irvin unharmed in Ed Hamilton's basement. Hamilton needed the ransom money to pay his business losses, but he picked the wrong man to kidnap.

The Case of the Organ-Grinder

When Tony was excited, he spoke too quickly and exchanged the first sounds of words.

He was excited when he told Sally the words the thief had on his T-shirt. He said, "Polar Bears."

Later, when Sally said "fired teet" for "tired feet," Encyclopedia realized what Tony had done. He had said "Polar Bears" when he had meant to say "Bowler Pairs."

The detectives had seen a boy with BOWLER PAIRS on his T-shirt scouting a candy counter.

They caught up with him at Mundy's Bakery.

He knew about Sally's punch, and after a few strong words from her, he returned Tony's money.

The Case of
Pablo's Nose

Desmoana denied being the girl whom Pablo had seen riding away on a purple bicycle.

To give herself an alibi, she claimed that her purple bicycle hadn't been ridden for nearly a year.

Encyclopedia had his doubts. So he got her to show off how well she rode a two-wheeler.

That was her mistake!

She couldn't have done tricks if the bicycle had really been unused for nearly a year. The tires would have lost air and been flat!

Pablo got his nose back. Since it was the only nose entered in the New Nose Now contest, it won.

SOLUTION TO
The Case of the Carousel Horse

Despite claiming he wasn't interested in making money, Mr. Jones hoped to sell Emperor as the work of R. A. Bently.

He carved Emperor himself. Since no photographs of Bently's horses existed, he thought he was safe.

He goofed, however. Because he was English, he put the picture of President Roosevelt and Bently's name above Emperor's left front leg.

That would have passed in England, where carousels turn clockwise. But in America carousels turn counterclockwise.

The *right* side of a figure turning counterclockwise faces the onlookers, not the left side!

After Encyclopedia pointed out the error, Pablo decided not to go to work for Mr. Jones.

The Case of the Wilford Whammy

The blond boy was Wilford's partner in the phony Whammy business. Encyclopedia knew it when Wilford made Fifi sit down with her chin up and head back.

In that position, her weight was mostly on the chair's seat, which became the center of gravity. For her to rise, the center of gravity had to shift to her feet.

That required her head to move forward. It couldn't, because Wilford was pushing the Whammy against her forehead.

The pushing—not some phony power—was holding her down. Wilford's finger would have worked as well!

When Encyclopedia explained this to the children, they took off for home.

The Case of the Racing Reptiles

Kid Tiger might have slipped through the bars of the cage and eaten Erasmus and Erastus. With both lizards inside him, however, he could not have squeezed back out.

When Encyclopedia pointed out his mistake, Barry confessed.

He didn't want Spike's Kid Tiger to win at the races. So he stole the snake and hid him.

He also hid Erasmus and Erastus to make it look as if Kid Tiger had eaten them. He planned to "find" the lizards before the races—and return Kid Tiger after the races.

It was all for nothing. On Saturday, Kid Tiger and Erasmus and Erastus failed to win a single race.

SOLUTION TO
The Case of the Unknown Thief

While standing at the counter, the thief overheard Mr. Rubin mention the value of Mr. Bower's watch.

Then the lights went out. The temptation was too much.

The thief swiftly found Mr. Bower's watch on the counter. In his eagerness to get away, he left his wallet and his wife's watch behind.

Encyclopedia told Mr. Bower to look for a *blind man*. The money in his wallet was the clue.

As Encyclopedia explained, folding bills according to value is a popular touch method used by blind people.

The blind thief was caught the next day.

About the Author

Donald J. Sobol is the award-winning author of more than sixty books for young readers. He lives in Florida with his wife, Rose, who is also an author. They have three grown children. The Encyclopedia Brown books have been translated into fourteen languages.

About the Illustrator

Eric Velasquez received his B.F.A. from the School of Visual Arts in New York City. He has exhibited his paintings and drawings at a number of galleries, including the Society of Illustrators, the Mussavi Art Center, the Ac-Baw Gallery, and the Greenberg Library. His illustrations have appeared in the Dojo Rats series by James Raven, and in Beverly Naidoo's books Chain of Fire and Journey to Jo'Burg, which was a Notable Children's Trade Book in the Field of Social Studies and won the Child Study Children's Book Committee Award. Mr. Velasquez lives in New York City.